# Little
# HORRORS

## Shiver with fear...

... shake with laughter!

D0522815

For Jack Morris
(*A Halloween boy!*)

Visit Shoo Rayner's website!
www.shoo-rayner.co.uk

| WALTHAM FOREST | |
|---|---|
| 026212802 | |
| PETERS | 22-Oct-07 |
| £3.99 | JF |
| | |

ORCHARD BOOKS
96 Leonard Street, London EC2A 4XD
*Orchard Books Australia*
Unit 31/56 O'Riordan Street, Alexandria, NSW 2015
First published in Great Britain in 2001
First paperback edition 2002
Copyright © Shoo Rayner 2001
The right of Shoo Rayner to be identified as the author
and illustrator of this work has been asserted by him in
accordance with the Copyright, Designs, and Patents Act, 1988.
A CIP catalogue record for this book is available
from the British Library.
ISBN 1 84121 636 4 (hardback)
ISBN 1 84121 644 5 (paperback)
1 3 5 7 9 10 8 6 4 2 (hardback)
7 9 10 8 6 (paperback)
Printed in Great Britain

# Little
# HORRORS
## The Pumpkin Man

Shoo Rayner

ORCHARD BOOKS

It was Halloween…

"Aaah!" screamed my sister, Kim.
"It's Dracula!"

"Don't be silly," I said. "It's only me."

Kim and I were dressed to go trick or treating.

Just as we were leaving, Miss Hitchens arrived.

"Hello, Sam," she said. "You do look scary. I *love* Halloween. It's so s-s-s-spooky!"

Miss Hitchens was pretty spooky herself. *She* wouldn't need to dress up to go trick or treating.

I hid behind Mum.

"Look!" Miss Hitchens cackled wildly.
"I've brought some pumpkin pie!"

"How kind of you," Mum said.
"Do come in. I'll make some coffee."

As Kim and I hurried out into the ice-cold darkness of the night, Mum called after us.

"Sam!" Kim whispered. "Everyone says Miss Hitchens is a witch. Do you think she really is?"

I thought about it, and shivered.

"There's no such thing as witches," I said, bravely. "Nor ghosts, nor monsters."

Just then, the hedge rustled,
and a giant monster leapt out
in front of us!

"S-A-A-A-M!" it moaned.

"Aaah!" I yelled.

The monster laughed. It was my friend, Jamie!

"Hur-hur!" he gurgled. "Tricked you!"

The rest of our friends crawled
out from the hedge. They were all
dressed up in Halloween costumes.
Now we were ready to spook our
neighbours!

We got a sweet from every house
we visited. So we didn't have to play
a trick on anyone. Soon our goody
bags were bursting!

Then Jamie said, "We've got our *treats*, now it's time for the *tricks* to begin!"

"What do you mean?" I said.

Jamie put on a spooky voice.
"It's time to get Old Hairy Witchens!"
he croaked. "Come on!"

My blood ran cold. Not creepy
Miss Hitchens.

"But...but..." I said.

Jamie shone the torch under his chin. The weird light made him look hideous.

"You're not *scared* are you?" he teased.

Soon, we were creeping up to Miss Hitchens's house.

Jamie pushed me towards the front gate. "Go on!" he hissed.

I clicked the latch.
Slowly, the gate opened.

We froze in fear. Had she heard us?

We tiptoed down the path to the front door.

A strange orange light glowed
behind the glass.

Jamie pushed me again. "Go on,"
he said. "Ring the bell."

I slowly raised my hand, and reached towards the bell…

Quickly, before I could change my mind, I pressed it.

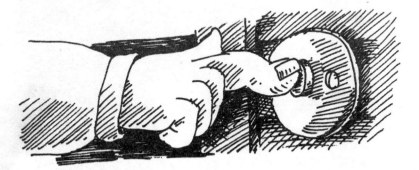

Nothing happened. Not a sound.

"Try knocking!" Jamie whispered.
I took a deep breath and touched
the heavy black doorknocker.

Slowly, ever so slowly, the door swung open.

Our eyes bulged in horror.

A pumpkin head was staring right at us. Its dagger-sharp teeth glinted in the orange glow.

Suddenly, the air was split by a
loud scream. Something black and
furry sprang out from the shadows.

We turned to run, stumbling and
bumping into each other.

But *something* was blocking
our path.

It was a giant pumpkin man!
Horrid, hollow laughter came
from its jagged mouth.

Its fingers wriggled and
twitched. They couldn't wait
to twist themselves around us!

The Pumpkin Man raised its
hands up high in the air,
and boomed loudly.

Here's a little
treat for you!

Something cold and slimy hit me,
slap in the face.

Kim grabbed my hand and we all ran to the back gate.

But it was stuck!

We were trapped!

The Pumpkin Man was coming across the lawn towards us. I could hear the rustle of its cloak, the swish of its long, creepy fingers.

It was getting closer…and closer…

Suddenly, the gate slammed open.

We all screamed, and tumbled into
the alleyway. Then we ran as fast
as we could, all the way home.

"At l-l-l-least we've got our treats," Kim panted, when we were safely back in our garden.

But our goody bag was torn. All the sweets had fallen out while we were running away, leaving a trail for the Pumpkin Man to follow…

"Come on," I said. "We'll be safe indoors."

I opened the back door - and my heart stopped.

There was Miss Hitchens.
"Hello dears," she smiled. "Did
you get some nice treats?"

"Oh, y-yes, thank you," we
stammered.

"You weren't *scared*, then?"
she said, grinning like a cat.

My bones turned to jelly as I
thought about the Pumpkin Man.

"I *love* Halloween," said Miss
Hitchens. "It's just a bit of fun, isn't it?"
She shrieked with laughter, and
something fell out of her frizzy,
ginger hair.

She picked it up and hid it in her pocket. But I'd seen what it was.

It was a pumpkin seed!
Had she been playing a Halloween trick on us? Or was she *really* a witch?

The next day, we saw Miss
Hitchens sweeping her pathway.

As we walked past, I swear her
black cat smiled at us – and winked!

Look out for these brilliant books from Orchard!

**Little Horrors by Shoo Rayner**

☐ The Swamp Man            1 84121 646 1
☐ The Pumpkin Man          1 84121 644 5
☐ The Spider Man           1 84121 648 8
☐ The Sand Man             1 84121 650 X

**Finger Clicking Reads by Shoo Rayner**

☐ Rock-a-doodle-do!        1 84121 465 5
☐ Treacle, Treacle, Little Tart   1 84121 469 8

**Grandpa Turkey's Tall Tales by Jonathan Allen**

☐ King of the Birds        1 84121 877 4
☐ And Pigs Might Fly       1 84121 710 7

**The One and Only by Laurence Anholt and Tony Ross**

☐ Micky the Muckiest Boy    1 86039 983 5
☐ Ruby the Rudest Girl      1 86039 623 2
☐ Harold the Hairiest Man   1 86039 624 0

*And many more!*